STELLA

FAIRY OF THE FOREST

MARIE-LOUISE GAY

ALLEN&UNWIN

This edition published in 2002

First published in Canada in 2002 by Groundwood Books Limited

Copyright © text and illustrations, Marie-Louise Gay 2002

Published in the UK in 2002 by
Allen & Unwin
PO Box 30474
London NW6 7FG
Phone: 44 0208 537 1531
Fax: 44 0208 621 3701

Published in Australia in 2002 by
Allen & Unwin
83 Alexander Street
Crows Nest NSW 2065
Australia
Phone: 61 2 8425 0100
Fax: 61 2 9906 2218
Email: info@allenandunwin.com
Web: www.allenandunwin.com

National Library of Australia Cataloguing-in-Publication entry:
Gay, Marie-Louise.
Stella, fairy of the forest.

For children aged 2 to 6 years.
ISBN 1 86508 751 3.

ISBN 1 86508 752 1 (pbk.).

I. Title.

813.54

Printed and bound in China.

10 9 8 7 6 5 4 3 2 1

To my father

"Stella!" called Sam. "Stella! Where are you?"
"Here," whispered Stella.

"Where?" said Sam. "I can't see you."
"That's because I'm practising to be invisible," said Stella.

"Now I see you," said Sam. "How did you do that?"
"I thought of invisible things," answered Stella, "like wind or music..."
"Or fairies?" asked Sam.

"Fairies aren't invisible," said Stella. "I've seen hundreds of them."
"Really?" said Sam. "Where did you see them?"
"In the forest," said Stella. "Over there. Let's go, Sam."

"I don't know," said Sam. "Are there any bears in the forest?"
"Bears sleep during the day," said Stella. "Come on, Sam."

"What do fairies look like?" asked Sam.
"They're tiny and beautiful," said Stella, "and they fly very fast."
"I see one!" said Sam. "Look!"

"That's a butterfly, Sam," said Stella.
"Do butterflies eat butter?" asked Sam.
"Yellow butterflies do," said Stella.

"Then I guess blue butterflies eat pieces of sky," said Sam.
"How do you know that?" asked Stella.
"I know a lot of things," said Sam.

"Look," said Sam, "some clouds just landed in that field."
"Those aren't clouds, Sam. They're sheep."
"Aren't sheep dangerous?" asked Sam.

"About as dangerous as woolly blankets," said Stella.
"Let's go say hello to them."
"You go," said Sam. "I'll just wave."

"Who planted all these flowers?" asked Sam.
"The birds and the bees," said Stella.
"Bees!" cried Sam. "Won't they sting us?"

"Not if you move ve-r-r-y slowly," said Stella.
"Stella?" said Sam. "You have a bee in your hair."
"Run, Sam, run!" cried Stella.

"We have to cross the stream," said Stella.
"I don't want to get my feet wet," said Sam.
"I'll carry you. Hop on!"

"Isn't it too slippery?" asked Sam. "Won't we fall in?"
"No, we won't," said Stella. "I'll walk on these rocks."
"Stella?" said Sam. "One of the rocks is moving."

"No, it isn't, Sam."
"Uh-oh…" said Sam.

"Was that a turtle, Stella?" asked Sam.
"Yes, Sam," sighed Stella.

"Isn't the forest beautiful?" said Stella. "Look at these big old trees."
"Are they older than Grandma?" asked Sam.
"Almost," said Stella. "They must be at least a hundred years old."

"Is that why their skin is so wrinkled?" asked Sam.
"That's not skin," said Stella. "That's bark."
"Grandma's bark is much softer," said Sam. "Especially on her cheeks."

"Climb up here, Sam," said Stella. "You can see the whole world."
"Can rabbits climb trees?" asked Sam.

"No, but you can," said Stella. "Come on, Sam. It's lovely up here."
"It's lovely down here, too," said Sam. "With the rabbits."

"Look, Sam," said Stella. "Isn't this a pretty snake?"
"It's pretty long," said Sam. "Don't snakes swallow people?"
"It's too small," said Stella.

"Maybe it only swallows small people," said Sam. "What's that?"
"A porcupine," said Stella. "Don't touch! It's very prickly."
"Why would anyone want to touch a porcupine?" said Sam. "Or a snake?"

"I'm the king of the castle," sang Stella.
"How do rocks grow so big?" asked Sam.
"A giant waters them every day," said Stella. "Come on up, Sam."

"I think the giant is watering his rocks right now," said Sam.
"It's just raining, Sam," said Stella. "Let's build a forest house."

"How?" asked Sam. "Why?"
"We'll make the roof out of branches and ferns," said Stella.
"And we'll sleep on a bed of moss."

"Sleep?" said Sam. "Won't the bears be waking up soon?"
"Just help me carry the ferns," said Stella.

"This is perfect," said Stella.
"What do we do now?" asked Sam.
"Look for fairies," said Stella. "If you see a fairy, you can make a wish."

"I see one!" cried Sam.

"Where? Where?"

"Too late!" said Sam. "It just flew away."

"Oh, well," said Stella. "What was your wish?"
"I wish I could stay here forever," said Sam.
"Me, too," said Stella.